Weekend with Grandmother

Weekend with Grandmother

By Wolfram Hänel

Illustrated by Christa Unzner

Translated by Martina Rasdeuschek-Simmons

North-South Books

NEW YORK • LONDON

Copyright © 2002 by Nord-Süd Verlag AG, Gossau Zürich, Switzerland
First published in Switzerland under the title *Ferien mit Oma*.
English translation © 2002 by North-South Books Inc., New York

First published in the United States, Great Britain, Canada,
Australia, and New Zealand in 2002 by North-South Books,
an imprint of Nord-Süd Verlag AG, Gossau Zürich, Switzerland.

Distributed in the United States by North-South Books Inc., New York.

Library of Congress Cataloging-in-Publication Data is available.
A CIP catalogue record for this book is available from The British Library.
ISBN 0-7358-1630-1 (trade edition) 10 9 8 7 6 5 4 3 2 1
ISBN 0-7358-1631-X (library edition) 10 9 8 7 6 5 4 3 2 1
Printed in Belgium

For more information about our books, and the authors and artists
who create them, visit our web site: www.northsouth.com

The last time Tony saw his grandmother
was four years ago.

Tony's grandmother lived in another
part of the country. And Tony's parents
were rather busy. When they had time, the
family usually drove to the seashore or the
mountains. But they never went to visit
Tony's grandmother.

In the past, Tony's grandmother had never complained. But one day a letter arrived from her:

I have had enough! If you won't come to visit, I will. But don't worry, I won't be a burden. I'll just pick up my grandson and take him on a short trip. And I'll pay for everything!

—Grandmother

"Grandmother has been acting a little strange lately," Tony's mother said.

Tony's father nodded and rolled his eyes.

When the day arrived, Tony stood at his window. Soon his grandmother would come and pick him up. Tony wasn't sure he really wanted to spend the whole weekend with her.

Suddenly a car stopped on the street below.

And what a car! It was a white convertible, with red leather seats.

Then Tony's eyes grew wide. Behind the wheel sat his grandmother!

She wore a straw hat, tied down with a
silk scarf.

"Grandmother is here!" shouted Tony, as he leaped down the stairs.

"Hello, my dears," said Grandmother. She handed Tony's mother a package. "This is for you," she said to Tony's parents. "In case you get bored while we're away." She winked at Tony.

In the package was a jigsaw puzzle.

"Well," said Mother, "a puzzle map of the country in a thousand pieces."

"I marked the town where I live with an X," said Grandmother. Then she grabbed Tony's bag and marched outside to the car.

"Did you pack your toothbrush?" asked Tony's mother. "Don't forget to eat regularly."

"Don't worry," Grandmother replied. She pointed to a basket of apples behind the front seat.

Tony grinned and jumped into the car.

"See you in two days!" Grandmother cried, as she started the engine.

"Drive carefully," called Tony's father.

Then Grandmother stepped on the gas.

"Where are we going?" asked Tony.

"No idea," said Grandmother. "We'll just drive for a while and when we find a place we like, we'll stop."

They took a winding
country road.

"Driving on the highway
isn't fun anymore," said
Grandmother. "Too crowded.
Here we are the kings of
the road."

Grandmother smiled as she drove. "This is a BMW V-8, you know," she told Tony. "A 1956 model. It's a classic. They don't make them like this anymore."

"It's great!" agreed Tony.

After a while, they got stuck driving behind a slow tractor.

"Get out of the way!" Tony called to the driver.

"What's the rush?" Grandmother replied. "We have all the time in the world."

Then she turned onto a dirt road and stopped beside a big green field.

"Lunchtime!" Grandmother announced.
She brought out a checked tablecloth.
Then a basket of food. She even had real
china dishes and silverware!

Tony and Grandmother sat in the sun
and enjoyed their meal. There were egg
salad sandwiches with watercress and crepes
with orange marmalade. There were fresh
rolls and three kinds of cheese and a big
salad, too. And for dessert, an apple for
Tony and coffee with a lot of sugar for
Grandmother.

22

"That's how your grandfather liked it,"
explained Grandmother, leaning back
comfortably.

Then she told Tony about the old days,
when his grandfather was still alive. And
Tony told her about school.

It was late afternoon when they packed
everything up and continued on their way.

"We should start looking for a place to
spend the night," said Grandmother.

Just then there was a loud bang,
followed by a clattering noise from the
engine.

The car came to a stop.

"Don't worry," said Grandmother. "It's only the fan belt again." She took out a pair of nylon stockings. "These should do the trick," she said.

Grandmother bent over the engine. Tony could hear her clinking and clanking. But she didn't complain—she even whistled a little song.

A car stopped. A man got out and asked if he could help.

But Grandmother said, "That's nice of you, young man. But I can take care of it myself."

It was getting dark when they arrived in
a small village. Grandmother parked in
front of an inn.

"We'll stay here," she said. She asked for
two rooms, one for her and one for Tony.

In the dining room, Grandmother studied the menu for a long time. She shook her head and frowned. Finally she said, "You know, I'm not really very hungry."

Tony was also full from the picnic. So they decided to skip dinner and go to bed.

Tony sat on his bed. He didn't know
what to think of his grandmother. She *was*
a little strange. His parents were right
about that. But on the other hand . . . well,
it seemed that she always knew exactly
what to do. She definitely knew a lot
about cars. And the picnic lunch was great.

Tony slid under the blanket and closed his eyes. He soon fell asleep. Suddenly he was wakened by a knock at the door. He sat up in alarm. When Tony opened the door, he saw a figure in a long white gown. At first he thought it was a ghost. But it was only Grandmother.

"Come with me," she whispered. "I have something to show you."

Grandmother took Tony's hand and pulled him down the hall and out onto the balcony. "Look at those stars," she said. "You never see them so clearly in the city."

As they watched a falling star, Grandmother told Tony a story about a woodpecker who pecked holes in the sky.

"And the lights we see through the holes are the stars," said Tony.

The next morning they set out bright
and early—before breakfast!

"We'll get something on the way," said
Grandmother.

Later they stopped at a bakery and
bought fresh rolls and hot chocolate.

At lunchtime they had another picnic, this time beside a small lake.

"Where will we go next?" asked Tony.

"Why don't we stay here for a while?" said Grandmother. "We can build a sand castle."

Grandmother pulled off her shoes and socks, rolled up her slacks, and waded into the water.

"It's a little cold," she called to Tony. "But you must try it!"

So Tony rolled up his pants and tiptoed into the cold water. Then they built a fantastic sand castle, with four towers and a moat.

Later, they lay on the checked tablecloth and watched the clouds pass overhead.

Time passed quickly. Soon it would be getting dark.

"I can't believe it's so late already," said Tony. "The day just flew by, even though we didn't really do anything."

"Wrong!" said Grandmother. "We did a lot of things. And now I'm hungry. Let's have dinner at a really fancy restaurant."

They drove through a big town, with lots of traffic. When they stopped at a red light, they saw an old man who seemed to be afraid to cross the street. Grandmother leaped out of the car and helped the old man cross.

The traffic light changed to green, and the cars behind them began to honk their horns impatiently. Tony was embarrassed.

But Grandmother grinned at him as she got back in the car. "Don't be embarrassed," she said. "Just imagine if you were that old man."

They found the best restaurant in town.
There was a candle on the table and soft
music played in the background.

Unfortunately, the waiter had given
them a table right next to a busy hallway.

"Excuse me," Grandmother said to the waiter. "Could we please have a different table?"

"I'm sorry," said the waiter. "It's impossible."

"But there are lots of other tables available," said Grandmother.

"Sorry," repeated the waiter, and he walked away.

"I believe they think we are not good enough for them," said Grandmother to Tony.

When the waiter returned with their salads, Grandmother said, "We would like to speak with the manager, please."

But the manager wasn't friendly either. "If you don't like the table, madam, perhaps you should leave."

Tony spoke up loud enough for everyone in the room to hear, "If we wanted to, we could buy this place, right, Grandmother?"

Everyone in the room was silent. Even Grandmother looked surprised. Then she winked at Tony and said to the manager, "My grandson is right. Perhaps *you* should start looking for a new job!"

And with that, Grandmother stood up and took Tony's hand. They marched out of the door.

Behind them, they heard the manager cry, "Wait, madam, please wait!"

When they reached the car, they burst out laughing. They laughed until they could hardly breathe.

"Now what?" asked Tony.

"Now we treat ourselves to some junk food, and then . . ." Tony's grandmother thought for a moment. "Then we are going to surprise your parents. I can't wait to see their faces when we knock on the door in the middle of the night. If they are already in bed, I'll just sleep on the sofa."

"Don't be silly," said Tony. "You can have my bed. I'll sleep on the sofa."

"It's a deal," said Grandmother.

It was nearly midnight when they got to Tony's house. But Tony's parents were still up. They were sitting on the living room floor with the jigsaw puzzle spread out in front of them.

"You're just in time to help us with a little problem," said Tony's mother. She pointed to the puzzle. "Look, we put it all together, but one piece is missing."

"Aha!" said Grandmother, taking a puzzle piece out of her pocket. It was the one with the X on it.

Tony's father quickly inserted the missing piece. Then he said, "By the way, we talked about something while you were gone. The next time we go on a trip, we thought we'd go here." He pointed to the puzzle piece with the X on it. "Of course, only if it's okay with you," he added, looking at Grandmother.

"Hooray!" cried Tony and threw his arms around Grandmother. Then he whispered to her, "We can go to the best restaurant and eat sandwiches brought from home, okay?"

"And if they don't like it," Grandmother said, "we'll just buy the place."

Then Tony and Grandmother joined hands, tossed their hats in the air, and danced around the room, laughing.

Tony's parents just looked at each other and shrugged. "Still a bit strange," said Tony's mother.

"But it's okay," said Tony's father.

About the Author

Wolfram Hänel was born in Fulda, Germany. He now divides his time between homes in Hannover, Germany, and a small village in Ireland. Among the other easy-to-read books he has written for North-South are *Abby, Rescue at Sea!*, *The Extraordinary Adventures of an Ordinary Hat*, and *Lila's Little Dinosaur*.

About the illustrator

Christa Unzner was born in Berlin, Germany. She worked in an advertising agency and is now a full-time freelance illustrator. Her other books for North-South include *Meredith, the Witch Who Wasn't, The Spy in the Attic, The Man with the Black Glove,* and *Loretta and the Little Fairy.*